this
little ORCHARD
book belongs to
....
....

D0453016

ORCHARD BOOKS
96 Leonard Street, London EC2A 4XD
Orchard Books Australia
32/45-51 Huntley Street, Alexandria NSW 2015
1 84362 215 7
First published in Great Britain in 1999
This edition published in 2003

A CIP catalogue record for this book is available from the British Library.
Printed in Italy

Freddie has a haircut

Nicola Smee

little ORCHARD

“It’s time for a haircut, Freddie!” says Mum.

It certainly is!

Bear wants to come
and watch.

“Hello Freddie! Hello Bear!”
says Bob, the hairdresser.

Bob is making my hair wet so that it's easier to cut.

I tell him to be careful not to snip my ears!

Snip
Snip

goo

All done!
Not bad!

"Here, pick a lollipop Freddie,
and take one home for Bear,"
says Bob.

Thank you Bob !

Bob's Hair Salon
Dad, can I have mine cut like Freddie's?

Freddie
you look LOVELY!